The Christmas Cottage Miracle

The Christmas Cottage Miracle

Matthew Petchinsky

The Christmas Cottage Miracle
By: Matthew Petchinsky

Introduction: A Cottage in the Snow

Deep within the heart of a snow-covered forest, where the frost clings to the boughs of ancient pines and the silence of winter hangs heavy in the air, a legend stirs. For centuries, travelers have whispered tales of a mysterious cottage that appears only on Christmas Eve. Tucked away amidst a landscape of untouched beauty, this enchanted dwelling is said to glow softly with a warm, golden light, its smoke curling lazily into the icy night sky. To the rare and fortunate souls who find it, the Christmas Cottage is more than a simple house; it is a gateway to miracles, a beacon of hope in the darkest season.

The origins of the Christmas Cottage are shrouded in mystery. Some say it was built by elves as a gift for the world, a place imbued with the magic of the North Pole itself. Others believe it to be the work of an ancient and benevolent spirit, who once walked the earth and left behind this sanctuary as a reminder of the goodness and generosity that can thrive even in the harshest winters. Whatever its origin, the cottage is not easily found. It reveals itself only to those whose hearts are pure, whose wishes are born of true need, and whose courage can withstand the trials of the snowy wilderness.

Legends describe the cottage as a wonder to behold. Its walls, crafted from logs of the finest spruce, are adorned with intricate carvings that seem to shift and dance in the flickering light of its windows. A garland of evergreen and holly drapes over the door, and the faint scent of cinnamon and pine lingers in the crisp air around it. Within its walls, time seems to stand still. A roaring fire warms the hearth, casting shadows that tell stories of old; a table, laden with the most sumptuous feast, waits to be shared. And yet, the cottage's greatest gift is not its comfort but its magic.

Those who have entered the Christmas Cottage speak of life-changing miracles—wounds healed, lost loved ones reunited, fears dispelled, and dreams fulfilled. But the miracles granted by the cottage are not without a cost. The wish must come from the depths of the heart, untainted by greed or malice. Those who seek its power with selfish intentions are said to find only an empty house, their footsteps the only sound in the otherwise silent woods. For the Christmas Cottage is no mere tool for desire; it is a place where love, hope, and redemption take root and flourish.

For as long as anyone can remember, the Christmas Cottage has been a source of inspiration and mystery. Parents tell their children stories of its wonders, encouraging acts of kindness and selflessness in the hopes of one day earning the cottage's favor. Poets and artists have tried to capture its magic, while adventurers have braved the winter wilds in search of it, often returning with tales of inexplicable warmth and light glimpsed through the snow—but never quite reaching it. It is said that the cottage chooses its seekers, appearing only to those who need it most, at the precise moment when its magic can change their lives forever.

As you step into the world of this tale, prepare to journey through a landscape as breathtaking as it is unforgiving, a place where the biting cold of winter is tempered by the warmth of hope. The story of the Christmas Cottage is one of love that transcends loss, of hope that endures in the face of despair, and of redemption that proves even the coldest hearts can thaw. It is a story for anyone who has ever wished upon a star, believed in the power of miracles, or dared to dream of a brighter tomorrow.

In the pages that follow, the mystery of the Christmas Cottage will unfold, drawing you into its spellbinding world. You will meet seekers whose lives hang in the balance, whose journeys through the snow-covered woods will test their resolve and transform their hearts. You will witness the cottage's magic at work, as it weaves its miracles and reveals the truths hidden within. And, perhaps, you will find a bit of its magic within yourself, a spark to carry forward into your own life.

The snow is falling. The forest awaits. And somewhere, in the depths of its wintry embrace, the Christmas Cottage stands, its golden light a beacon of hope in the darkness. The journey begins now.

Chapter 1: A Wish in the Storm

The wind howled through the small town of Pinebrook, rattling windows and piling drifts of snow against the doors of every house. For Sarah, the biting cold of winter was nothing compared to the chill of her own worries. As a single mother, she had grown accustomed to scraping by, stretching every dollar and every ounce of energy to provide for her seven-year-old daughter, Lily. But this Christmas Eve, the struggle felt heavier than ever.

Sarah had made a decision—a desperate one. With her meager savings nearly gone and no gifts to brighten Lily's holiday, she had resolved to visit her estranged father. The relationship had been fractured for years, but the hope of reconciliation, combined with the chance of a better future for Lily, pushed her forward. Clutching a worn map and bundled against the cold, Sarah loaded Lily into their aging station wagon and began the journey through the snowy woods.

The drive was treacherous. Snow fell in thick, swirling sheets, obscuring the road ahead. The old car groaned in protest, its tires struggling to grip the icy surface. Lily sat quietly in the back seat, her small hands clutching a tattered stuffed rabbit. She watched the snow with wide eyes, sensing her mother's tension but saying nothing.

When the blizzard intensified, Sarah's heart sank. The wind roared like a living thing, buffeting the car until it felt as though they were driving through a sea of white chaos. Suddenly, the engine sputtered and died, leaving them stranded in the middle of nowhere. Panic surged through Sarah as she tried and failed to restart the car. They were miles from the nearest town, with no cell service and no sign of another vehicle on the deserted road.

"Mommy, what do we do now?" Lily's voice was small and frightened.

Sarah forced a brave smile. "We'll be okay, sweetheart. Let's see if we can find shelter." She grabbed their coats, a flashlight, and a blanket, bundling Lily up as much as she could before stepping out into the storm.

The woods loomed dark and unwelcoming, their snow-laden branches creaking ominously. Sarah carried Lily, trudging through the knee-deep snow, her legs burning with effort. The cold seeped into her bones, and each step felt heavier than the last. She whispered silent prayers for guidance, for a miracle to save them from the unforgiving storm.

And then she saw it.

Through the swirling snow, a faint golden light flickered in the distance. At first, Sarah thought her eyes were playing tricks on her. But as she drew closer, the light grew brighter, steady and inviting. There, nestled among the trees, stood a small cottage. Its windows glowed warmly, and smoke curled from its chimney, a beacon of comfort in the frozen wilderness.

"Look, Lily! A house!" Sarah's voice broke with relief as she quickened her pace.

They reached the door, and Sarah hesitated for only a moment before knocking. The wood felt warm under her knuckles, as though the cottage itself were alive. The door creaked open, revealing an interior that seemed to radiate magic. A roaring fire crackled in the hearth, and the scent of cinnamon and pine filled the air. The walls were adorned with evergreen garlands, and a table was set with an inviting feast.

But there was no one there.

Sarah stepped inside, the warmth enveloping her like a soft embrace. She set Lily down and closed the door behind them. "Hello?" she called, her voice trembling.

No answer came. Yet, the cottage did not feel abandoned. It felt... expectant, as though it had been waiting for them.

Sarah sank into a chair by the fire, holding Lily close. For the first time in hours, she allowed herself to hope. Whatever this place was, it had saved them. And as she gazed into the dancing flames, a single thought took root in her heart: perhaps this Christmas Eve held more than survival. Perhaps it held a miracle.

Chapter 2: The Secrets of the Cottage

The warmth of the Christmas Cottage embraced Sarah and Lily like a long-lost friend, but the comfort only deepened the mystery. As Lily napped under a knitted blanket by the hearth, Sarah began to explore. The cottage, though small, was a treasure trove of curiosities. Shelves lined the walls, filled with books, trinkets, and jars of herbs that gave off faint, comforting scents. Everything seemed untouched by time, as if the cottage had been preserved in a bubble of enchantment.

On a small table near the window, Sarah found an old leather-bound journal. Its cover was embossed with an ornate symbol that seemed to shimmer faintly in the firelight. Intrigued, she opened it and began to read. The journal was a collection of entries written by previous visitors to the cottage. Each page told a different story—a tale of a miracle granted and a life forever changed.

One entry, written in elegant script, described a farmer who had stumbled upon the cottage during a brutal drought. The cottage had given him the knowledge to find a hidden spring on his land, saving his family and their livelihood. Another entry, penned in shaky handwriting, recounted the story of a young woman who had lost her sight. After a night in the cottage, she awoke with her vision restored. Each story was different, yet they all carried the same message: the cottage was a place of miracles.

But as Sarah read on, a recurring theme began to emerge. Each miracle came with a personal sacrifice. The farmer had to leave his land to ensure the spring's water would never be overused. The young woman had to forfeit her ability to speak in exchange for her sight. The journal's final pages held a warning, written in bold, underlined text:

"The cottage grants miracles only to those whose hearts are true, but no gift comes without a price. Consider carefully what you ask for, for the cost may be greater than you are prepared to pay."

Sarah's heart raced as she closed the journal. What could she possibly ask for that wouldn't cost more than she was willing to give? Her eyes drifted to Lily, who slept peacefully, her small face illuminated by the firelight. Sarah knew that her daughter's happiness and safety were her only priorities, but the journal's warning lingered in her mind.

As she continued to explore, Sarah noticed something unusual about the cottage. It seemed to respond to her thoughts and emotions. When she felt a pang of worry, the fire crackled brighter, as if to reassure her. When she thought of Lily, the scent of vanilla cookies filled the air, reminiscent of the treats her daughter loved. The cottage's magic was subtle but undeniable, and it seemed to be urging her to trust it.

In the kitchen, Sarah found a tray of warm pastries and a pot of hot cocoa, as though someone had prepared them just moments before. She hesitated, then took a cautious bite. The food was delicious, filling her with a warmth that went beyond the physical. It was as if the cottage knew exactly what she needed.

Despite the cottage's comforts, Sarah couldn't shake the feeling that she was being tested. The journal's warning loomed large in her mind, and she wondered what kind of sacrifice she might be asked to make if she dared to wish for a miracle. As the night wore on, Sarah sat by the fire, the journal in her lap, and wrestled with the weight of her decisions. Somewhere in the depths of her heart, a wish began to form, but she knew that whatever she asked for, it would come at a cost.

The cottage's secrets were many, but one thing was clear: its magic was as complex as it was powerful. As Sarah drifted into an uneasy sleep, she couldn't shake the feeling that the real test had only just begun.

Chapter 3: A Test of Faith and Love

The air in the cottage seemed to hum with anticipation as Sarah sat by the ancient wooden table, her hands trembling as they clutched a steaming cup of tea. She stared into the swirling liquid as though the answer to her problems would materialize within its depths. The walls of the cottage creaked softly, almost as if they were alive, breathing in time with the magic that coursed through the space.

Suddenly, the air grew still, and a figure stepped into the dim light of the room. He appeared as if from nowhere, a tall, ethereal man with kind, weathered eyes and a flowing robe that shimmered like starlight. His presence exuded a quiet power, commanding respect without instilling fear.

"I am Nicholas," the figure said, his voice as soft and warm as a fireside glow. "The guardian of this place. It is rare for travelers to find this cottage, rarer still for those who do to face the choice you must make."

Sarah's breath hitched, and she set her cup down carefully. "A choice?" she asked, her voice tinged with both awe and trepidation.

Nicholas nodded. "The cottage holds an ancient power. It grants miracles, but only when the wish is born from true selflessness. This is a place of purity, Sarah. It will see through any shadow of greed or selfish intent. You must choose carefully."

The weight of his words settled heavily on Sarah's shoulders. For months, she had fought against a tide of financial ruin and personal despair. The thought of wishing for wealth, for a reprieve from the relentless struggle, was almost irresistible. Yet, the image of her daughter, Lily, with her radiant smile and boundless imagination, tugged at her heart.

"What if I don't know what to wish for?" Sarah asked, her voice trembling. "What if... I make the wrong choice?"

Nicholas stepped closer, his gaze steady. "The right choice will not come from your mind, but your heart. The cottage will know if your wish is true."

The Enchanted Room

Meanwhile, in another corner of the cottage, Lily wandered down a narrow hallway that seemed to stretch endlessly, though the cottage appeared small from the outside. The walls were lined with carvings of trees and stars, intricate and ancient. At the end of the hallway, she found a small wooden door with a brass handle that gleamed like gold.

Curious, she turned the handle and stepped inside. The room was bathed in a soft, otherworldly glow. On one wall, a mirror hung, but it did not reflect the present. Instead, it showed moving images—scenes from the past, their family's past.

Lily gasped as she saw her mother and father laughing together in a bright, sunlit field, Lily herself a baby in their arms. But the images shifted, showing arguments, tears, and a moment when her father stormed out, leaving Sarah crumpled on the floor, holding Lily close.

Tears pricked Lily's eyes as she watched these memories play out. She had always sensed the pain her mother carried, but now she saw it in vivid detail. She touched the mirror, and it seemed to pulse under her fingertips.

"Why are you showing me this?" she whispered to the room.

The cottage, alive with its own magic, seemed to answer in the way the images slowed, focusing on Sarah's face. The message was clear: Lily was meant to understand her mother's sacrifices, her resilience, and the love that had kept them going despite everything.

Confronting the Past

Lily ran back to find her mother, bursting into the main room where Sarah and Nicholas stood. "Mom," she cried, her voice urgent. "I saw it! The cottage... it showed me everything!"

Sarah turned, alarmed at the distress in her daughter's voice. "What do you mean, sweetheart?"

"The mirror," Lily said, pointing down the hallway. "It showed me... us. What happened with Dad. All the times you cried when you thought I wasn't looking. All the times you chose me over everything else."

Sarah's eyes filled with tears, and she reached for Lily, pulling her close. The memories were a wound she had tried to bury, but now they were laid bare for both of them.

Nicholas watched silently, allowing the moment to unfold. Finally, he spoke. "Sarah, the test is not about the wish itself. It is about whether you can face your truth, let go of the past, and trust in love."

Sarah looked at her daughter, her heart aching with both pride and pain. The choice became clear in that moment.

"I wish for Lily's happiness and health," she said firmly, her voice steady despite the tears on her cheeks. "I wish for her to have a life full of joy and love, even if it means I must keep struggling."

The Miracle

The cottage seemed to sigh in relief, its magic wrapping around them like a warm embrace. Nicholas smiled, his form beginning to fade.

"You have chosen well, Sarah," he said. "The cottage will honor your wish, not only for Lily but for you, too. True selflessness is always rewarded."

As Nicholas disappeared, the cottage seemed to transform. The once-crumbling walls became pristine, the air filled with the scent of blooming flowers. And for the first time in months, Sarah felt a deep sense of peace, knowing that the love she had for her daughter was the strongest force of all.

In the enchanted room, the mirror now reflected only the present—a family healing, together, ready to face whatever came next.

Chapter 4: The Miracle's Price

The moment Sarah uttered her wish, the cottage seemed to come alive with an otherworldly energy. The walls shimmered as though veiled in starlight, and the air was thick with the scent of blooming flowers and ancient wood. A warm glow enveloped Sarah and Lily, a tangible manifestation of the magic that resided within the cottage.

Sarah felt a surge of hope, but it was quickly tempered by an unsettling sensation, as though a shadow had crept into the room. The light began to flicker, the warmth giving way to an icy chill. Nicholas, the guardian of the cottage, reappeared, his expression no longer serene but grave.

"Sarah," Nicholas said, his voice carrying both compassion and weight, "your wish has been accepted. Lily will have a life filled with love, joy, and security. But every miracle demands a price, and this one is no different."

Sarah's heart sank. "What do you mean? What price?"

Nicholas stepped closer, his gaze piercing. "The magic of this place is not without balance. For Lily's wish to come true, you must let go of the dream you have carried in your heart—the dream of reconciling with your father."

A Dream Shattered

The words hit Sarah like a physical blow. Ever since her father had walked out of their lives when she was a teenager, she had harbored a quiet hope that one day they would find their way back to each other. She had imagined long conversations, apologies exchanged, and a future where her father could be a part of her and Lily's lives.

"But... why?" Sarah asked, her voice trembling. "What does my father have to do with this?"

Nicholas sighed, his expression softening. "The cottage knows your heart, Sarah. It knows the weight of your past, the pain you carry, and the hope that keeps you tethered to it. For Lily's future to be secure, you must release the chains of your past. Holding on to the dream of reconciliation divides your energy and focus. Letting it go will allow you to fully embrace the life you have now."

Tears welled in Sarah's eyes. "I've waited so long for him to come back. For him to tell me why he left, to apologize. How can I just let that go?"

Nicholas's voice softened. "The past cannot be rewritten, Sarah. Your father made his choices, and you must make yours. True miracles require sacrifice—not to punish, but to free you. If you cling to what was, you may miss what could be."

Confrontation and Reflection

The room grew quiet as Sarah struggled with the enormity of the decision. Lily, sensing her mother's distress, approached and wrapped her arms around her waist.

"Mom," Lily whispered, "you don't have to do anything you don't want to. But... I don't need anyone but you."

Sarah looked down at her daughter, her heart breaking and healing all at once. She thought about the nights she had stayed awake, replaying memories of her father, and the mornings she had woken up to Lily's laughter. One was a ghost, a haunting, while the other was a vibrant, living force of love.

"Will I ever see him again?" Sarah asked Nicholas, her voice barely above a whisper.

"That is not for the cottage to decide," Nicholas replied. "But the dream of reconciliation—the one where everything is healed and perfect—must be surrendered. Only then can the magic work fully, and only then can you find peace."

Sarah closed her eyes, tears streaming down her cheeks. The pain was raw, but beneath it, she felt a small, steady flame of resolve.

"I let go," she said finally, her voice trembling but firm. "I let go of the dream. If it means Lily will have everything she needs, I'll let it go."

The Price is Paid

As soon as the words left her lips, the cottage responded. The flickering light steadied, becoming a radiant glow that filled every corner of the room. The icy chill dissipated, replaced by a warmth that seemed to seep into Sarah's very soul.

The walls shimmered with images of Sarah's life—not her father, but moments of strength and love she had created for herself and Lily. The first time Lily called her "Mommy," the laughter they shared over burnt pancakes, the quiet nights reading stories by candlelight. The images were a reminder that while her father's absence had left a scar, it had not defined her life.

Nicholas watched, his expression both proud and wistful. "You have chosen wisely, Sarah. The cottage's magic is complete. Lily's future is secure, and now, so is yours. The miracle is not just for her—it is for both of you."

A New Beginning

The cottage settled into a quiet calm, the magic fading back into the fabric of the space. Sarah felt a strange lightness, as though a weight she had carried for years had finally been lifted. She looked down at Lily, who was smiling up at her, and she realized that for the first time in a long while, she was truly present in the moment.

"Thank you," Sarah said to Nicholas, her voice filled with gratitude.

He smiled, beginning to fade once more. "The miracle is yours to carry forward, Sarah. Love and joy will flourish, but remember: the price you paid is a reminder to cherish what you have. The past is a shadow; the future is your light."

As Nicholas disappeared, Sarah and Lily stood together in the cottage, now filled with a quiet, steady peace. The miracle had come, and with it, a lesson that would guide Sarah for the rest of her life: sometimes, to gain the future, you must let go of the past.

For Sarah, the price had been steep, but the reward—a life filled with love and possibilities—was worth every tear.

Chapter 5: A Christmas Reunion

The sound of chirping birds and the faint rustle of melting snow greeted Sarah and Lily as they stirred awake. The storm that had raged with such ferocity the previous night was gone, leaving a serene winter wonderland in its wake. Sarah rubbed her eyes, her breath visible in the crisp morning air, and realized they were no longer in the magical Christmas Cottage.

She sat up slowly, taking in her surroundings. They were outside, nestled in a clearing surrounded by snow-dusted pines. Ahead of them was a small, modest house with a red front door and a single, flickering porch light. Smoke curled from the chimney, promising warmth and comfort inside.

"Mom?" Lily's sleepy voice broke the silence.

Sarah turned to her daughter, brushing snowflakes from her golden hair. "I don't know where we are, sweetheart," she said softly. "But it feels... familiar."

Then, as though the universe had orchestrated it, the red door swung open. A man stepped onto the porch, his figure tall and slightly stooped, his face lined with age and the weight of years gone by. Sarah's breath caught in her throat. It was her father.

The Miracle's Revelation

"Sarah?" he called, his voice rough but unmistakably filled with emotion. "Is that really you?"

Sarah froze, her heart pounding. She had spent years imagining this moment, though she had given up hope of it ever happening. Now, standing before her was the man who had left when she was still a teenager, the man whose absence had shaped so much of her life.

"Dad," she whispered, tears welling in her eyes.

He moved quickly, almost stumbling in the snow, until he was standing before them. His eyes searched hers, taking in every detail, as though he couldn't quite believe she was real. Then his gaze shifted to Lily, and a soft smile broke across his weathered face.

"This must be Lily," he said, his voice trembling. "She looks just like you did at her age."

Lily glanced up at Sarah, unsure but curious. "Mom, who is he?"

Sarah knelt beside her daughter, her hands gently resting on Lily's shoulders. "This is your grandfather," she said, her voice cracking.

A Healing Conversation

The three of them moved inside, where a warm fire crackled in the hearth. The house was simple, with mismatched furniture and the scent of cinnamon and pine lingering in the air. It was cozy, a stark contrast to the emotional distance Sarah had felt from her father for so many years.

Over steaming mugs of cocoa, Sarah and her father began to talk. At first, the words came slowly, haltingly. He explained why he had left—a mixture of personal failures, fear, and the belief that they would be better off without him. He admitted his mistakes, his regrets, and how he had spent years searching for a way to make things right but never knew how to approach her.

"I was wrong, Sarah," he said, his voice heavy with remorse. "I thought I was doing what was best, but I see now that I only caused pain. I've dreamed of this moment for so long, but I never imagined it would actually happen."

Sarah listened, her emotions a whirlwind of anger, sadness, and a cautious hope. She spoke of her struggles, the years of feeling abandoned, and the strength she had found in raising Lily on her own.

"I've been so angry with you for so long," she admitted, tears streaming down her face. "But part of me always hoped you'd come back."

Her father reached for her hand, his own trembling. "I can't change the past, but I want to be here now—for you and for Lily. If you'll let me."

The Cottage's Legacy

As the conversation unfolded, Sarah felt a weight lift from her heart. The dream of reconciliation that she had surrendered in the Christmas Cottage had not been for nothing. The miracle had worked in ways she hadn't expected, not erasing the past but creating the opportunity for a new beginning.

When the time came to step outside, they found the landscape transformed. The Christmas Cottage was gone, as if it had never existed. In its place stood a single glowing lantern resting atop the snow, its light steady and warm.

"What's that, Mom?" Lily asked, pointing to the lantern.

Sarah approached it slowly, picking it up and holding it in her hands. The lantern's glow seemed to pulse gently, as though alive. She knew in her heart it was the cottage's way of saying good-bye—a reminder of the magic that had brought them here.

"It's a gift," Sarah said softly. "A reminder of the miracle we've been given."

Christmas Morning

As the first light of Christmas morning broke through the trees, Sarah, Lily, and her father stood together on the porch, watching the sunrise. The world was bathed in hues of gold and pink, the snow sparkling like diamonds.

For the first time in years, Sarah felt whole. The fractures of the past had not disappeared, but they had been mended with love, forgiveness, and hope.

"Merry Christmas," her father said, his voice thick with emotion.

"Merry Christmas," Sarah replied, her arm around Lily, who snuggled close.

The three of them stood there, united by the miracle that had brought them together. The future was uncertain, but for now, they had each other—and that was enough.

As the sun rose higher, the lantern's glow began to fade, its job complete. But in Sarah's heart, the light of the Christmas Cottage would burn forever, a beacon of love and the magic of second chances.

Appendix A: The Legend of the Christmas Cottage

The Christmas Cottage, shrouded in mystery and steeped in legend, is a beacon of magic and hope. Throughout the centuries, this enchanted structure has appeared to those in dire need, often in the midst of snowstorms or during moments of profound despair. Its origins are as enigmatic as its miracles, whispered about in folktales and passed down through generations.

The Origins of the Christmas Cottage

The precise origins of the Christmas Cottage remain unknown, but its story is rooted in ancient lore. Some believe the cottage was created by a benevolent spirit of the winter solstice, a being who wished to bring warmth and light to those enduring the darkest nights. Others say it is a gift from Saint Nicholas himself, a manifestation of his desire to spread love and selflessness during the holiday season.

The first recorded mention of the Christmas Cottage dates back to the early 13th century, when a monk traveling through the Alps claimed to have been rescued by a glowing structure that appeared in the midst of a blizzard. The monk later described the cottage as a place of divine power, where he was granted the strength to forgive a grievous betrayal by a fellow brother.

Over the centuries, the cottage has been depicted in countless stories and paintings, always described as a cozy, snow-covered haven with glowing windows and a faint scent of pine and cinnamon.

The Rules of the Christmas Cottage

The Christmas Cottage is not an ordinary house; it operates according to its own mystical rules. These rules ensure that the miracles it grants are born of purity and selflessness, reinforcing its role as a place of transformation and healing.

1. **The Wish Must Be Selfless:**
   The cottage only grants miracles when the wish stems from a place of genuine selflessness. Greedy or selfish desires will be rejected, and the cottage may disappear entirely if the visitor's heart is not true.

2. **A Test of Faith and Love:**
   Visitors are often tested before their wish is granted. These tests may involve confronting fears, releasing long-held resentments, or making difficult sacrifices. The cottage seeks to ensure that the miracle granted aligns with the visitor's true needs, not merely their wants.

3. **The Miracle's Price:**
   Every miracle requires a price, often in the form of letting go of something from the past. This is not a punishment but a means of creating balance and opening the visitor's heart to new possibilities.

4. **The Cottage Chooses Its Visitors:**
   The cottage does not appear to just anyone. It seeks out those who are at a crossroads in their lives, those who carry heavy burdens but possess the potential for profound change.

Tales of Other Visitors

The Christmas Cottage has touched the lives of many over the centuries, each encounter leaving behind a tale of transformation and hope. Here are a few of the most enduring stories:

The Farmer's Sacrifice

In the late 1800s, a struggling farmer named Thomas stumbled upon the cottage during a harsh winter. His crops had failed, and his family was starving. Thomas was given a choice: wish for wealth to secure his farm or wish for his son to find happiness and success, even if it meant losing the farm. He chose his son's happiness, and though the farm was lost, his son went on to become a renowned inventor, eventually bringing prosperity to the entire family.

The Widow's Redemption

In the 1940s, a grieving widow named Eleanor found herself at the cottage's door. She had spent years harboring anger toward her late husband for secrets revealed after his death. The cottage presented her with a mirror that showed her husband's true intentions, allowing her to see his love and sacrifices in a new light. Forgiving him, she found peace and was able to reconnect with her estranged children.

The Orphan's Wish

In the 1970s, a young boy named Daniel, who had been abandoned at a snowy train station, was guided to the cottage by a mysterious light. Daniel wished for a family, and though the cottage did not bring his biological parents back, it led him to a kind couple who adopted him. They later credited their decision to an inexplicable urge to visit the station that night.

Lessons from the Cottage

Each encounter with the Christmas Cottage leaves behind lessons that resonate long after the miracles are granted. Some of the most profound include:

- The Power of Letting Go: True peace often comes from releasing the past and embracing the present.
- The Strength in Selflessness: Acts of genuine love and selflessness are the foundation of meaningful miracles.
- The Importance of Faith: Believing in the possibility of change can open the door to transformation.

The Glowing Lantern

One of the most enduring symbols of the Christmas Cottage is the glowing lantern it often leaves behind. This lantern serves as a reminder of the magic and lessons experienced by its visitors. It is said that the lantern's light never fades, symbolizing the eternal nature of hope, love, and selflessness.

The Christmas Cottage may vanish as mysteriously as it appears, but its impact endures. For those who are fortunate enough to cross its threshold, it is a place of profound transformation, a testament to the enduring magic of faith, love, and the human spirit.

Appendix B: The Guardian's Wisdom

Nicholas, the enigmatic guardian of the Christmas Cottage, serves as both protector and guide for those who stumble upon its magical refuge. His presence is a blend of warmth and authority, offering wisdom and insight to those seeking the miracles the cottage can bestow. Though his origins remain a mystery, his reflections and teachings resonate with a timeless truth, embodying the essence of the cottage's purpose.

This appendix collects Nicholas's advice, reflections on selflessness and sacrifice, and excerpts from a journal believed to belong to him—a text discovered by a past visitor to the cottage. These words offer a deeper understanding of the cottage's magic and the transformative power of Christmas miracles.

The Nature of Selflessness

One of Nicholas's central teachings revolves around the concept of selflessness. To him, selflessness is not merely an act but a way of being—a conscious decision to prioritize the well-being of others over one's own desires, even when it demands great personal sacrifice.

"True selflessness is not about denying your needs," Nicholas once explained to a visitor. "It is about recognizing that the joy and well-being of others are intrinsically tied to your own. When you give without expecting anything in return, you create a ripple of love and kindness that transforms the world around you."

He often encouraged visitors to look beyond their immediate struggles and consider the greater good. For Nicholas, selflessness was the foundation upon which the miracles of the Christmas Cottage were built.

The Power of Sacrifice

Nicholas understood that the path to miracles often required letting go. Sacrifice, he taught, was not about loss but about making space for something greater.

"To sacrifice is to release the weight of what no longer serves you," he wrote in his journal. "It is not a punishment but an opportunity—a chance to grow, to heal, and to embrace the possibilities of the future."

Nicholas believed that every sacrifice, no matter how painful, carried within it the seeds of renewal. He saw sacrifice as a bridge between the past and the future, a way to reconcile old wounds while making room for new blessings.

"Clinging to the past," he told a grieving visitor, "is like holding onto a tree branch while the river of life carries you forward. You must let go if you wish to move with the current."

The True Meaning of Christmas Miracles

For Nicholas, the miracles of the Christmas Cottage were not simply magical occurrences but profound moments of transformation and clarity. He believed that miracles were the natural result of faith, love, and selflessness working in harmony.

"A miracle is not a gift from the heavens," he wrote. "It is the manifestation of love in its purest form. It is what happens when we open our hearts, trust in the unseen, and choose to act with compassion."

Nicholas often reminded visitors that miracles were not about material rewards but about emotional and spiritual growth.

"Do not look for a miracle to solve your problems," he advised. "Look for a miracle to guide you toward the answers that already lie within your heart."

Excerpts from Nicholas's Journal

The following passages are taken from a weathered journal discovered in the Christmas Cottage by a visitor in the 19th century. Though its authorship cannot be confirmed, the writings align closely with the teachings attributed to Nicholas.

On Love and Forgiveness

"Love is the greatest force in the universe, but it is also the most fragile. To love is to risk pain, but it is through that pain that we grow. Forgiveness is love's highest form—an act of courage that liberates both the giver and the receiver."

On Facing Fear

"Fear is the shadow of the unknown, a specter that feeds on doubt. But fear is also a teacher. When we confront it, we discover our strength, and in that strength, we find the courage to choose love over despair."

On the Magic of Christmas

"Christmas is not a single day nor a collection of traditions. It is a state of being, a moment when humanity remembers its capacity for kindness and hope. The magic of Christmas lies in the hearts of those who dare to believe in miracles—not as gifts but as acts of love."

The Guardian's Final Reflection

In his final entry, Nicholas left a message for those who would one day find the journal:

"The cottage is not the source of miracles—you are. It merely reflects the light within you, the love you are capable of giving and receiving. Every test, every sacrifice, is a step toward uncovering the truth of who you are. Believe in yourself, believe in others, and let the spirit of Christmas guide you."

The Legacy of Nicholas's Wisdom

Though the Christmas Cottage appears only briefly in the lives of its visitors, the wisdom of Nicholas lingers, etched into the hearts of those he has touched. His teachings remind us that the greatest miracles are not found in material wealth or fleeting desires but in the strength to love, forgive, and embrace the unknown.

Through his guidance, the magic of the Christmas Cottage becomes more than a legend—it becomes a testament to the enduring power of faith, selflessness, and the human spirit.

<u>Message from the Author:</u>

I hope you enjoyed this book, I love astrology and knew there was not a book such as this out on the shelf. I love metaphysical items as well. Please check out my other books:

-Life of Government Benefits

-My life of Hell

-My life with Hydrocephalus

-Red Sky

-World Domination:Woman's rule

-World Domination:Woman's Rule 2: The War

-Life and Banishment of Apophis: book 1

-The Kidney Friendly Diet

-The Ultimate Hemp Cookbook

-Creating a Dispensary(legally)

-Cleanliness throughout life: the importance of showering from childhood to adulthood.

-Strong Roots: The Risks of Overcoddling children

-Hemp Horoscopes: Cosmic Insights and Earthly Healing

- Celestial Hemp Navigating the Zodiac: Through the Green Cosmos

-Astrological Hemp: Aligning The Stars with Earth's Ancient Herb

-The Astrological Guide to Hemp: Stars, Signs, and Sacred Leaves

-Green Growth: Innovative Marketing Strategies for your Hemp Products and Dispensary

-Cosmic Cannabis

-Astrological Munchies

-Henry The Hemp

-Zodiacal Roots: The Astrological Soul Of Hemp

- **Green Constellations: Intersection of Hemp and Zodiac**

-Hemp in The Houses: An astrological Adventure Through The Cannabis Galaxy

-Galactic Ganja Guide

Heavenly Hemp

Zodiac Leaves
Doctor Who Astrology
Cannastrology
Stellar Satvias and Cosmic Indicas
<u>Celestial Cannabis: A Zodiac Journey</u>
AstroHerbology: The Sky and The Soil: Volume 1
AstroHerbology:Celestial Cannabis:Volume 2
Cosmic Cannabis Cultivation
The Starry Guide to Herbal Harmony: Volume 1
The Starry Guide to Herbal Harmony: Cannabis Universe: Volume 2

Yugioh Astrology: Astrological Guide to Deck, Duels and more
Nightmare Mansion: Echoes of The Abyss
Nightmare Mansion 2: Legacy of Shadows
Nightmare Mansion 3: Shadows of the Forgotten
Nightmare Mansion 4: Echoes of the Damned
The Life and Banishment of Apophis: Book 2
Nightmare Mansion: Halls of Despair
<u>Healing with Herb: Cannabis and Hydrocephalus</u>
<u>Planetary Pot: Aligning with Astrological Herbs: Volume 1</u>
Fast Track to Freedom: 30 Days to Financial Independence Using AI, Assets, and Agile Hustles
<u>Cosmic Hemp Pathways</u>
How to Become Financially Free in 30 Days: 10,000 Paths to Prosperity
Zodiacal Herbage: Astrological Insights: Volume 1
Nightmare Mansion: Whispers in the Walls
The Daleks Invade Atlantis
Henry the hemp and Hydrocephalus

10X The Kidney Friendly Diet
Cannabis Universe: Adult coloring book
Hemp Astrology: The Healing Power of the Stars

Zodiacal Herbage: Astrological Insights: Cannabis Universe: Volume 2

<u>**Planetary Pot: Aligning with Astrological Herbs: Cannabis Universes: Volume 2**</u>

Doctor Who Meets the Replicators and SG-1: The Ultimate Battle for Survival

Nightmare Mansion: Curse of the Blood Moon

<u>**The Celestial Stoner: A Guide to the Zodiac**</u>

Cosmic Pleasures: Sex Toy Astrology for Every Sign

Hydrocephalus Astrology: Navigating the Stars and Healing Waters

Lapis and the Mischievous Chocolate Bar

Celestial Positions: Sexual Astrology for Every Sign

Apophis's Shadow Work Journal: : A Journey of Self-Discovery and Healing

Kinky Cosmos: Sexual Kink Astrology for Every Sign

Digital Cosmos: The Astrological Digimon Compendium

Stellar Seeds: The Cosmic Guide to Growing with Astrology

Apophis's Daily Gratitude Journal

Cat Astrology: Feline Mysteries of the Cosmos

The Cosmic Kama Sutra: An Astrological Guide to Sexual Positions

Unleash Your Potential: A Guided Journal Powered by AI Insights

Whispers of the Enchanted Grove

Cosmic Pleasures: An Astrological Guide to Sexual Kinks

369, 12 Manifestation Journal

Whisper of the nocturne journal(blank journal for writing or drawing)

The Boogey Book

Locked In Reflection: A Chastity Journey Through Locktober
Generating Wealth Quickly:
How to Generate $100,000 in 24 Hours
Star Magic: Harness the Power of the Universe
The Flatulence Chronicles: A Fart Journal for Self-Discovery
The Doctor and The Death Moth
Seize the Day: A Personal Seizure Tracking Journal
The Ultimate Boogeyman Safari: A Journey into the Boogie World and Beyond

Whispers of Samhain: 1,000 Spells of Love, Luck, and Lunar Magic: Samhain Spell Book

Apophis's guides:

Witch's Spellbook Crafting Guide for Halloween

<u>Frost & Flame: The Enchanted Yule Grimoire of 1000 Winter Spells</u>

<u>The Ultimate Boogey Goo Guide & Spooky Activities for Halloween Fun</u>

Harmony of the Scales: A Libra's Spellcraft for Balance and Beauty
The Enchanted Advent: 36 Days of Christmas Wonders

Nightmare Mansion: The Labyrinth of Screams

Harvest of Enchantment: 1,000 Spells of Gratitude, Love, and Fortune for Thanksgiving

The Boogey Chronicles: A Journal of Nightly Encounters and Shadowy Secrets

The 12 Days of Financial Freedom: A Step-by-Step Christmas Countdown to Transform Your Finances

Sigil of the Eternal Spiral Blank Journal

A Christmas Feast: Timeless Recipes for Every Meal

Holiday Stress-Free Solutions: A Survival Guide to Thriving During the Festive Season

Yu-Gi-Oh! Holiday Gifting Mastery: The Ultimate Guide for Fans and Newcomers Alike

Holiday Harmony: A Hydrocephalus Survival Guide for the Festive Season

Celestial Craft: The Witch's Almanac for 2025 – A Cosmic Guide to Manifestations, Moons, and Mystical Events

Doctor Who: The Toymaker's Winter Wonderland

Tulsa King Unveiled: A Thrilling Guide to Stallone's Mafia Masterpiece

Pendulum Craft: A Complete Guide to Crafting and Using Personalized Divination Tools

Nightmare Mansion: Santa's Eternal Eve

Starlight Noel: A Cosmic Journey through Christmas Mysteries

The Dark Architect: Unlocking the Blueprint of Existence

Surviving the Embrace: The Ultimate Guide to Encounters with The Hugging Molly

The Enchanted Codex: Secrets of the Craft for Witches, Wiccans, and Pagans

Harvest of Gratitude: A Complete Thanksgiving Guide

Yuletide Essentials: A Complete Guide to an Authentic and Magical Christmas

Celestial Smokes: A Cosmic Guide to Cigars and Astrology

Living in Balance: A Comprehensive Survival Guide to Thriving with Diabetes Insipidus

Cosmic Symbiosis: The Venom Zodiac Chronicles

The Cursed Paw of Ambition

Cosmic Symbiosis: The Astrological Venom Journal

Celestial Wonders Unfold: A Stargazer's Guide to the Cosmos (2024-2029)

The Ultimate Black Friday Prepper's Guide: Mastering Shopping Strategies and Savings

Cosmic Sales: The Astrological Guide to Black Friday Shopping

Legends of the Corn Mother and Other Harvest Myths

Whispers of the Harvest: The Corn Mother's Journal

The Evergreen Spellbook

| 38 | –

The Doctor Meets the Boogeyman

The White Witch of Rose Hall's SpellBook

The Gingerbread Golem's Shadow: A Study in Sweet Darkness

The Gingerbread Golem Codex: An Academic Exploration of Sweet Myths

The Gingerbread Golem Grimoire: Sweet Magicks and Spells for the Festive Witch

The Curse of the Gingerbread Golem

10-minute Christmas Crafts for kids

<u>Christmas Crisis Solutions: The Ultimate Last-Minute Survival Guide</u>

Gingerbread Golem Recipes: Holiday Treats with a Magical Twist

The Infinite Key: Unlocking Mystical Secrets of the Ages

Enchanted Yule: A Wiccan and Pagan Guide to a Magical and Memorable Season

Dinosaurs of Power: Unlocking Ancient Magick

Astro-Dinos: The Cosmic Guide to Prehistoric Wisdom

Gallifrey's Yule Logs: A Festive Doctor Who Cookbook

The Dino Grimoire: Secrets of Prehistoric Magick

The Gift They Never Knew They Needed

The Gingerbread Golem's Culinary Alchemy: Enchanting Recipes for a Sweetly Dark Feast

A Time Lord Christmas: Holiday Adventures with the Doctor

Krampusproofing Your Home: Defensive Strategies for Yule

Silent Frights: A Collection of Christmas Creepypastas to Chill Your Bones

Santa Raptor's Jolly Carnage: A Dino-Claus Christmas Tale

Prehistoric Palettes: A Dino Wicca Coloring Journey

The Christmas Wishkeeper Chronicles

The Starlight Sleigh: A Holiday Journey

Elf Secrets: The True Magic of the North Pole

Candy Cane Conjurations

Cooking with Kids: Recipes Under 20 Minutes

Doctor Who: The TARDIS Confiscation
The Anxiety First Aid Kit: Quick Tools to Calm Your Mind
Frosty Whispers: A Winter's Tale
The Infinite Key: Unlocking the Secrets to Prosperity, Resilience, and Purpose
The Grasping Void: Why You'll Regret This Purchase
Astrology for Busy Bees: Star Signs Simplified
The Instant Focus Formula: Cut Through the Noise
The Secret Language of Colors: Unlocking the Emotional Codes
Sacred Fossil Chronicles: Blank Journal

If you want solar for your home go here: https://www.harborso-lar.live/apophisenterprises/

Get Some Tarot cards: https://www.makeplayingcards.com/sell/ apophis-occult-shop

Get some shirts: https://www.bonfire.com/store/apophis-shirt-emporium/

Instagrams:
@apophis_enterprises,
@apophisbookemporium,
@apophisscardshop
Twitter: @apophisenterpr1
Tiktok:@apophisenterprise
Youtube: @sg1fan23477, @FiresideRetreatKingdom
Hive: @sg1fan23477
CheeLee: @SG1fan23477

Podcast: Apophis Chat Zone: https://open.spotify.com/show/ 5zXbrCLEV2xzCp8ybrfHsk?si=fb4d4fdbdce44dec

Newsletter: https://apophiss-newsletter-27c897.beehiiv.com/

If you want to support me or see posts of other projects that I have come over to: **<u>buymeacoffee.com/mpetchinskg</u>**
I post there daily several times a day

Get your Dinowicca or Christmas themed digital products, especially Santa Raptor songs and other musics. Here: **https://sg1fan23477.gumroad.com**

Apophis Yuletide Digital has not only digital Christmas items, but it will have all things with Dinowicca as well as other Digital products.

www.ingramcontent.com/pod-product-compliance
Lightning Source LLC
Chambersburg PA
CBHW061726130726
47996CB00006B/2522